The Case of the Fiendish Dancing Footprints

Sherlock Hound

Make friends with the most famous dog detective in town!

 Be sure to read:

The Case of the Disappearing Necklace

The Case of the Howling Armour

The Case of the Giant Gulping Bluebells

... and lots, lots more!

The Case of the Fiendish Dancing Footprints

Karen Wallace

illustrated by Emma Damon

M SCHOLASTIC

To Jane, who's always on the case – K.W.

Scholastic Children's Books,
Commonwealth House, 1-19 New Oxford Street,
London, WC1A 1NU, UK
a division of Scholastic Ltd
London ~ New York ~ Toronto ~ Sydney ~ Auckland
Mexico City ~ New Delhi ~ Hong Kong

First published by Scholastic Ltd, 2002

Printed and bound by Oriental Press, Dubai, UAE

10 9 8 7 6 5 4 3 2 1

Chapter One

Sherlock Hound, famous dog detective, stepped forwards and backwards then twirled around in a graceful circle. The sound of waltz music filled the air.

His loyal assistant, Dr WhatsUp Wombat, shook his head unhappily.

"I'll never get it," he muttered.

"Of course you will," said Sherlock Hound. He moved around the floor again. "One, two, three, turn. One, two, three, turn. Now you try."

"One, two, three..." murmured Dr WhatsUp Wombat. There was a thud and a crash as he banged into a table and knocked over a chair.

Sherlock Hound lifted up the record needle on the old-fashioned gramophone and the waltz music stopped.

"You'll never learn to dance if you don't turn," he muttered.

"I keep forgetting," wailed Dr WhatsUp
Wombat.

"I know," said Sherlock Hound. He
looked around the room and tried not to
growl. "Most of the furniture is broken."

"Shall I try one more time?" asked
Dr WhatsUp
Wombat
hopefully.

Before Sherlock Hound could bark "NO!"
there was a knock on
the door.

A man
holding an
envelope
stepped into
the room.
"Top Secret
Telegram,"
he said.

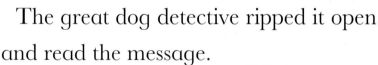

The great dog detective ripped it open
and read the message.

EMERGENCY!
Dr GreyMatter and the
GreyMatter Gadget
have disappeared!
Come to my office
immediately.

Sir Sid Whisper —
Head of the Secret
Service

Sherlock Hound put on his travelling cloak and ran down the stairs.

"I shall call a taxi, Dr WhatsUp," he cried. "Hurry! There's no time to lose!"

Chapter Two

Sherlock Hound and Dr WhatsUp Wombat
opened the door of the Secret Service
building and ran inside.

"What do you know about Dr GreyMatter?" Sherlock Hound asked his loyal assistant.

"He invented the GreyMatter Gadget, he has a parrot called Birdbrain and they both eat cheese and pickle sandwiches," replied Dr WhatsUp Wombat.

"What's special about the GreyMatter Gadget?" asked Sherlock Hound.

Dr WhatsUp Wombat shrugged. "It's so secret, hardly anyone knows."

Sir Sid Whisper's office was on the top floor.

They jumped into the lift and shot upwards.

Sir Sid Whisper leaned across his desk. He was a big fat man with a big fat problem. "Can you keep a secret?" he whispered.

"Of course," replied Sherlock Hound.

"The GreyMatter Gadget can read people's minds," said Sir Sid Whisper. "If it got into the wrong hands, the world would be in BIG trouble." He wiped his forehead with a sweaty handkerchief. "Imagine! There would be no such thing as a secret any more!"

"Is the GreyMatter Gadget very complicated?" asked Sherlock Hound.

Sir Sid Whisper nodded. "Fiendishly difficult. Only Dr GreyMatter knows how to work it."

"Where was Dr GreyMatter last seen?" asked Sherlock Hound.

"At his laboratory, sharing a cheese and pickle sandwich with his parrot," said Sir Sid Whisper.

Sherlock Hound thought hard. "Lock your door and don't leave your office," he said.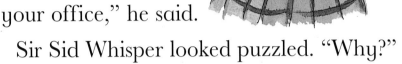

Sir Sid Whisper looked puzzled. "Why?"

"Because you could be in danger," replied Sherlock Hound. "As head of the Secret Service you know more secrets than anyone else. And the GreyMatter Gadget could find out every single one."

Sir Sid's face went as white as a piece of chalk.

Chapter Three

Two hours later Sherlock Hound and
Dr WhatsUp Wombat stood outside
Dr GreyMatter's laboratory.

They had never seen so many high walls,
locks and bars in all of their lives. It looked
more like a fortress than a laboratory.

"No one could ever break in here," muttered Dr WhatsUp Wombat. "So Dr GreyMatter couldn't have been kidnapped."

Sherlock Hound nodded. "Someone must have lured him away."

He stared at a concrete path that led to the front door. A sign read WET CEMENT. But the path was covered in footprints.

KEEP OUT

Keep Off
Wet
Cement

Sherlock Hound bent down and examined the footprints more closely.

They seemed to be facing forwards and backwards – almost as if someone had been dancing.

Then he saw something that made his stomach turn to ice.

In front of the footprints were pawprints.

Hyena pawprints!

Dr WhatsUp Wombat's eyes went as round as saucers. "Professor Ha-ha Hyena!" he gasped.

"Exactly!" cried Sherlock Hound. "Master of disguise and the most evil criminal in the world!"

Dr WhatsUp Wombat looked up at the fortress in front of them. "But how could he have got inside?" he croaked.

Before Sherlock Hound could answer, a huge grey parrot fluttered out of the laboratory window and perched on the sign in front of them.

"It's Birdbrain," whispered Dr WhatsUp.
Birdbrain cocked his head and stared at
Sherlock Hound with his clever yellow eyes.

He flapped his wings and began to
whistle a very strange tune.

Then something extraordinary happened!
Both Sherlock Hound and Dr WhatsUp
Wombat started dancing.

"I can't stop!" gasped Dr WhatsUp
Wombat.

"Nor can I!" puffed Sherlock Hound.

At last Sherlock Hound clapped
his paws hard. "Stop!"
he shouted.

When Birdbrain stopped
whistling, Sherlock Hound and Dr
WhatsUp Wombat stopped dancing!

"What on earth is going on?" gasped
Dr WhatsUp Wombat.
"Why did that
tune make
us dance
like that?"

"Easy peasy," replied the great dog detective. "It's just like the Pied Piper in the fairy tale. Professor Ha-ha Hyena must have played an irresistible tune on a pipe – that's how he lured Dr GreyMatter from his laboratory."

Dr WhatsUp Wombat went pale. "We should warn Sir Sid Whisper right away."

Chapter Four

Too late!

By the time Sherlock Hound and Dr WhatsUp Wombat returned to the Secret Service building, Sir Sid Whisper had disappeared!

All that was left were footprints in his sandpit.

"What on earth was he doing in a sandpit?" asked Dr WhatsUp Wombat.

"Having top secret meetings," explained Sherlock Hound. "No one would ever think to find him there, except..."

The great dog detective looked cunning. "We must track down that evil hyena straight away," he said. "And I know just how to do it!"

"How?"

"With a cheese and pickle sandwich," replied Sherlock Hound firmly.

Inside a tree house, completely hidden by leaves, Professor Ha-ha Hyena kissed his reflection in the lid of the GreyMatter

Gadget. "Soon I shall be very, very rich."

"Oh no you won't!" cried Dr GreyMatter from the other side of the tree house. "I'll never show you how to work my Gadget."

"So you'll never get my secrets!" gasped Sir Sid Whisper, who was slumped beside him.

"Is that so?" replied Professor Ha-ha Hyena. He picked up his pipe. "Perhaps after a couple more dances you'll change your minds."

Poor Dr GreyMatter and Sir Sid Whisper! From the moment the evil hyena began to play, they couldn't stop themselves dancing!

Chapter Five

Outside Dr GreyMatter's laboratory, Sherlock Hound opened a paper bag and took out a huge cheese and pickle sandwich. Then he handed Dr WhatsUp Wombat two round, pink lumps.

"I don't like pink
sweets," said Dr
WhatsUp Wombat.

"They're not
sweets. They're
earplugs," said Sherlock Hound. "Put them
in your pocket. You'll need them later."

At that moment, Birdbrain fluttered down
beside them. He watched as Sherlock
Hound put the cheese and pickle sandwich
into a tiny basket. It had a handle just big
enough for a parrot to carry.

Because Sherlock Hound had a plan!
Dr GreyMatter and his parrot always ate
their cheese and pickle sandwiches together,
so Birdbrain would lead them to his master.

As Birdbrain picked up the basket in his
beak, Sherlock Hound
tied a cotton bag
to his left foot.

It had a tiny hole in it and it was full of
white rice. All they had to do was follow the
trail of grains.

Back in the tree house, Sir Sid Whisper and Dr GreyMatter were lying flat out on the floor. They were so tired out from dancing, they could hardly speak.

"All right," gasped Dr GreyMatter. "I'll show you how to work the Gadget."

Sir Sid Whisper could only nod.

"I'm glad you've decided to see it my way," cried Professor Ha-ha Hyena. He threw back his head and let out a cry of bloodcurdling laughter.

Dr GreyMatter got up and slowly crossed the room to where the GreyMatter Gadget sat on a table.

"Hurry up!" snarled the evil Hyena. "I've got secrets to sell!"

With a very unhappy look on his face,
Sir Sid Whisper sat down on a chair while
Dr GreyMatter fixed a pair of wires to his
head, a clip to his nose
and two shiny, gold
headphones to his ears.

Chapter Six

Sherlock Hound stared at the trail of white rice. It stopped at the bottom of a ladder propped up against a tree. He looked up and his heart thumped in his chest.

Hidden among the leaves was a tree house!

At that moment,
Birdbrain fluttered
down from the
branches and
landed on the
top of the ladder.

Sherlock Hound turned to his loyal
assistant. "The evil hyena's hiding up there,"
he whispered.
"It's time to
surprise him."

He put in his
earplugs and
began to climb
the ladder.

Dr WhatsUp Wombat felt for his own
earplugs. But his
pockets were
empty. The
earplugs must
have fallen out!

He took a deep
breath and
slowly followed
the great dog
detective up
the ladder.

Sherlock Hound peered through the
tree house window.
What he saw
made his
stomach
turn over.

Sir Sid Whisper
was plugged into
the GreyMatter
Gadget and he
seemed to be talking like mad.

They were too late!

Then Sherlock
Hound saw Professor
Ha-ha Hyena half-
asleep on his
chair.

What on earth was going on?

The great dog detective took out an earplug and listened hard.

"And then when I was three years old I put the toffee in my pocket and I didn't tell ANYONE," wailed Sir Sid Whisper.

Sherlock Hound nearly burst out laughing. Sir Sid Whisper was telling his secrets, all right.

But he was starting at the very beginning!

"Can't you speed it up?" snapped
Professor Ha-ha Hyena at Dr GreyMatter.
As he spoke he noticed a parrot sitting on
the window sill with a basket in
his beak.

Suddenly Professor Ha-ha Hyena
felt his nose twitch.
Once to the left,
three to the right.
There was
only one smell
that made
his nose do that!
HOUND! *SHERLOCK* HOUND!

The evil hyena grabbed the GreyMatter
Gadget.

"Not so fast, Professor!" barked Sherlock
Hound. He stuffed in his earplug and
jumped through the window.

Dr WhatsUp Wombat jumped through
after him.

"Fancy a dance?" cried the evil hyena. With his other hand he put his pipe to his lips and began to play as fast as he could. Everyone except Sherlock Hound started hopping around the tree house like crazy.

It was impossible for Sherlock Hound to get through!

Suddenly
there was
a terrible
splintering noise.

"The tree house is
breaking! The tree house is breaking!"
squawked Birdbrain.

As Sherlock Hound dashed across the
floor, Professor Ha-ha Hyena dropped
everything and leaped through the window.

"Flea-ridden
mutt!" he cried.
"You'll never catch
me now!"

A second later, the tree house crashed down and everyone, except the evil hyena, tumbled on to the ground.

Back at 221b Barker Street, waltz music filled the air. Sherlock Hound stepped forwards and backwards and twirled in a graceful circle.

Dr WhatsUp Wombat danced beside him.

And this time there wasn't a single piece of broken furniture anywhere.

"See!" said Sherlock Hound. "I knew you'd get it."

Dr WhatsUp Wombat looked puzzled. "It was something to do with all that dancing in the tree house."

He sighed. "But if I hadn't lost my earplugs we might have caught the professor."

"Never mind," said the great dog detective kindly. "We've got the GreyMatter Gadget and as for that evil hyena, we'll get him next time." Sherlock Hound held out his paws and smiled. "Care for a dance?"